The Ballad Of Kulakoonstru

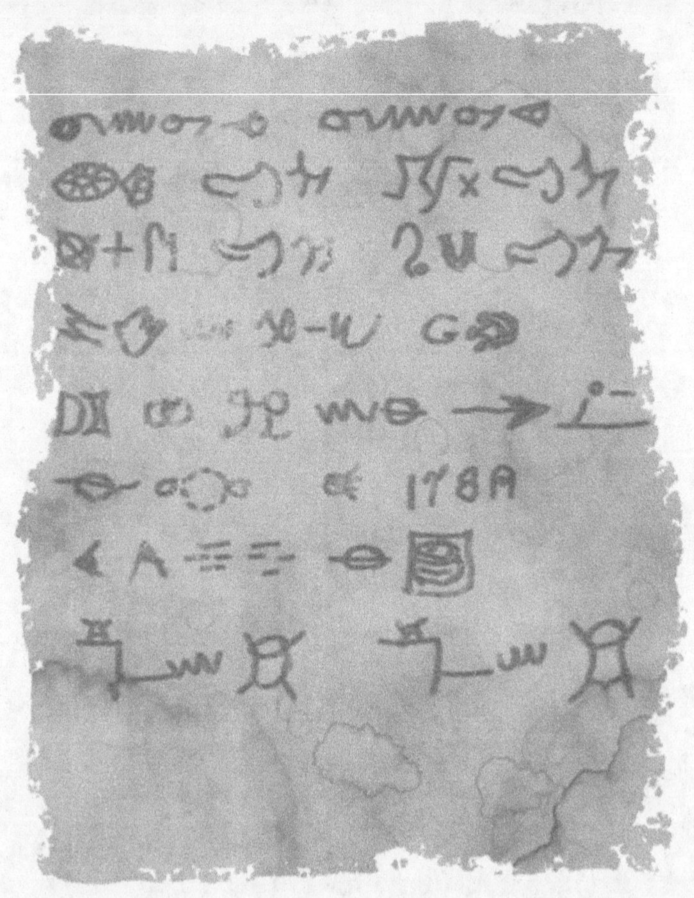

Facsimile of a surviving canto refrain page

The Ballad of Kulakoonstru

Edited By
Ukunhururarklo

Translated from the Yanin By
Dr. Robert R. Clinton, Ph.D.

University of Arqnasquirg Press
Airë Silanarfarnë *Arqnasquirg*

The Ballad of Kulakoonstru

ISBN: 978-1-61469-069-6
e-book ISBN: 978-1-61469-068-9

Second edition

Dedicated to all the Oids, Oid Types, Oidettes and Stupid Oids that I have adventured with over the years.

Contents

Translator's Note:

This text was originally published for a Yanin audience, many centuries ago. As such, some of the references may not be familiar to our modern English readers. The editorial decision was made to leave all references intact, as intended for the Yanina reader.

It is hoped that English readers will be able to discern most of the meanings and enjoy the published work as intended.

One additional note, in the ancient tongue, "Yanin", the two syllable word describing the language and Kulakoonstru's species, is more properly pronounced as a three syllable word, best approximated as "Yanina". This is supported by the rhyming scheme as seen in the ancient text. In this publication, we will use this ancient version, "Yanina".

Dr. Robert R. Clinton
Minneapolis, Minnesota
USA

The Text of The Ballad Of Kulakoonstru

Historical Introduction

This manuscript was found in one of the most ancient temples of Silanarë, in the main city of the Yanina: Arqnasquirg. But the text dates much further back than the founding of the temple to Silanarë.

The manuscript was discovered by a Yanina scholar, during his search for historical artifacts and records that were from the pre-Silanarë era, when the Yaninas worshipped Angle Sou, the old Death God, among the other ancient gods. The temple to Silanarë had been constructed on the site of an ancient Death God temple. This scholar, named Ukunhururarklo, was sifting through the various parchment and vellum records in the chambers under the temple, in what used to be the main repository for some of the more precious Death God records.

Ukunhururarklo came across a sealed chest, about the size of a quarter cask of whisky. The seal was unfamiliar to him, the language was not modern Yanina and he didn't recognize it immediately. He could make out the crest that he thought belonged to the legendary Kulakoonstru*.

The chest was a find of immense importance, both to the temple of Silanarë and Yaninas in general. The chest was taken to the high priest, who consulted various other Yanina scholars and clergy before they decided to carefully open it.

---

*There are multiple accepted spellings of the name within the academic community, including the archaic Yanina variant of "Kulakoonstroo". In this publication, we use the more modern spelling of "Kulakoonstru" throughout.

Inside they found several scrolls, sealed with crumbling wax seals. The scrolls were deteriorating, due to age and also because it appeared that beer or whisky may have been spilled on them more than once. In addition to the scrolls, a statue of a Yanina, thought to be Kulakoonstru himself, was inside. It was thought that this statue once had magical powers, and would speak Kulakoonstru's various titles to those passing by it. There was also a very faded cylinder seal.

A special room in the temple was designated for scholars to handle these scrolls with the utmost care. The statue itself was given a place of high honor in the temple of Silanarë, though unfortunately the magic was not recoverable because it was mana-based.

The scrolls were slowly unrolled and copied on to fresh parchment as they were examined. Sadly some of the text was totally unreadable, but much was salvageable. It was clear that at least one entire scroll was either missing or had utterly disintegrated to dust. Then came the next task: translate the scrolls into modern Yanina. For it was found to be written in a very ancient version of Yanina, which was not well understood by the peoples of this time.

The team of scholars worked diligently to copy and translate the scrolls. Ukunhururarklo was put in charge of conducting the translation and preparing the text for initial publication. His original notes are given as a preface, and also the occasional footnote in the text itself.

The scrolls, now properly known as "The Ballad Of Kulakoonstru", tell the story of the life of the legendary Yanina Kulakoonstru, who's deeds still echo so many thousands of years later in the hearts and mind of Yaninas and others worldwide.

Preface to the Revised Second Edition of The Ballad Of Kulakoonstru

This second edition, published some thirty-five years after the discovery of these legendary scrolls, contains some revised text as well as some newly determined passages.

Originally, there were some passages in Canto IV (where Kulakoonstru and his unnamed human companion journey to Slar Nk Grna, which is unpronounceable and is more commonly known as the Elven dungeon) that were so badly spilled on I could not initially make them out. There were also several smaller sections that I was unable to discern as well, usually for the same reason. I chose to publish the first edition with those verses simply left blank and noted this in the text.

This may have been in error. Canto IV describes one of the rather critical junctures of the story, when Kulakoonstru became the Close, Personal Friend of the Death God. This part was almost wholly unreadable due to several major stains on the original scroll. This left some significant gaps in the knowledge of the life of this remarkable Yanina.

Extensive study of the manuscript continued after the publication of the first edition. Close attention was paid to those illegible passages that were obscured by stray spills of whisky or beer. Usually these were deciphered with much difficulty as I learned more about the subject and became more facile with the ancient tongue. A little whisky should not impede Yanina scholarship!

As for Canto IV, with help from other extant historical sources found in the original temple of the Death God in Old Arbeneth, and some judicious detective work on the original section of the scroll containing Canto IV, I was able to piece together how these momentous events happened and determine most of the damaged verses. But it was not a speedy process.

There are still cantos that are completely missing or nearly so. These have been summarized in the text as best as possible, based on the available information from other sources about the life of Kulakoonstru. In those cases, canto breaks have been inferred from existing cantos and how they were originally structured.

Based on feedback from scholars and casual readers alike, I have added line numbers to this edition as convenient references. Along with some other text corrections and emendations, I present in this second edition, the most complete and authoritative version of The Ballad of Kulakoonstru.

The Honorable Ukunhururarklo
Chair, Department of Kulakoonstru Studies
Airë Silanarfarnë

Preface to the First Edition of The Ballad Of Kulakoonstru

It is my great privilege to present as complete a copy of The Ballad of Kulakoonstru that we know of in our time. By way of a brief introduction, Kulakoonstru, one of the most well known and powerful Yaninas, lived several thousand years ago, in a time before our great and powerful god Silanarë assumed the mantle of his godhood.

Kulakoonstru was of a class of Yaninas known as the "adventurer", meaning he (we shall designate him "he" since his actual sex remains unknown) was not part of the general mercenary class of warrior Yaninas that were prevalent then and now. He would go out with a few non-Yanina companions and seek glory and treasure. As the following tale shows, he found a great deal of both.

I am unsure who composed this epic ballad. It is written is an archaic style, even considering the age of the language itself. It appears that the scrolls were all written by the same hand, so these were either copied from earlier disparate sources, or written by a single author. The language appears to be contemporaneous to Kulakoonstru, and so I conclude it was written by a single person, possibly someone who personally knew him.

While it is possible that Kulakoonstru himself composed this, it seems unlikely given that his ultimate fate remains unknown. Rumor has it that he relocated to an upper plane, where he lives to this day, possibly with the mysterious Elves. But since it is no longer possible for even the gods to travel to the upper planes, this is pure conjecture for the moment.

The poem is broken up into multiple cantos, separated by a chorus describing only some of the various titles of the illustrious Kulakoonstru. This was a common way to tell epic tales in ancient times, it allowed for an oral tradition whereby the history could be memorized by even the smallest of Yaninas. It is generally expected that an epic lay such as this be shouted out as loudly as possible. Usually accompanied by prodigious quantities of beer or whisky, which may account for some of the damage to the scrolls.

Not all the cantos survived the unrolling or the unfortunate prior damage from some kind of liquid (more than likely the aforementioned whisky or beer). It also seems probable that one or more scrolls are completely missing, which is clearly a great loss to our scholarship.

It is obvious from this text that Kulakoonstru was a great and worthy Yanina, most certainly the greatest of his Age. All of his titles were inscribed on the cylinder seal that was found along with the scrolls and the now non-magical statue of him.

I have striven to present this with as close to the original meaning as possible, some ancient words have been re-translated and other concepts clarified. But whenever possible the words used are original, as is the rhyming and the meter. I have used minimal annotations, simply to avoid interrupting the flow of what is a classic story told by a master bard.

And now, for your enjoyment and edification, I present to you, The Ballad of Kulakoonstru!

Ukunhururarklo
Scholar of Ancient Yanina History
Temple of Silanarë, Arqnasquirg

The Ballad Of Kulakoonstru

Kulakoonstru! Kulakoonstru!
Diamond Wielder! Tech Wielder!
Ability Wielder! Lithon Wielder!
Supplier of Clarth's Petroni!
Close, Personal Friend of the Death God!
The Unseen! Time Traveler!
Shadow Walker! The Good!
Lord of Yaninas! LORD OF YANINAS![1]

I

Awesome Kulakoonstru, born[2] to
The most noble Yanina house.
Too darn cute was Kulakoonstru,
Stealthy and silent as a mouse.
The Incredible One was raised
A great Lord of Yaninaland.
His instructors were all amazed
By his fleet feet and his quick hand.

---

[1] The inter-canto chorus is a partial listing of Kulakoonstru's titles. His known titles number several more, and were inscribed on a cylinder seal which was found with the scrolls. See the appendix for the full list of known titles. See frontispiece for a facsimile of a chorus page.

[2] It is unclear precisely when Kulakoonstru was born because of his extensive time traveling (note his title: Time Traveler). References to him are spread throughout Yanina history, but the last was several thousand years prior to the ascension of the gods. It is assumed he was born in Arqnasquirg, as most Yanina were then and still are today.

He grew to full Yaninahood.
He made his decision to fight,
He was sure no one ever would
Withstand his mastery and might.
Leaving his old homeland behind,
Sailing ‘cross seas and oceans blue,
To the dwellings of humankind[3].
Where he could see all that was new.
Yaninas are all apexes,
They are the greatest of beings.
Puny humans, just two sexes,
On only one side be seeing!
Yaninas can fight all the foes.
Humans are always defeated!
They can barely keep on their toes,
Yaninas are unimpeded!
Squirg cannot be downed by humans,
At least not in enough amounts,
They even give instruction in
How to safely drink just an ounce![4]
And when they drink Yanina beer,
They are knocked flat on their backside.
Yanina look at them and sneer:
"Silly human, have you no pride?"
They can't walk in the bright sunlight,
Yaninas are unaffected.
Beer does not diminish their might
They are e'er calm and collected!

---

[3] These dwellings are now known as Old Arbeneth and the various cities surrounding it. At the time, there were enclaves of Yaninas in several of these cities.

[4] This is not an exaggeration! Even today, the authorities in Old Aberneth publish a pamphlet advising humans on how to "safely" drink squirg. It is highly amusing. See: Yanina Squirg: How To Safely Imbibe. Old Aberneth Government Publication.

From one tavern to the next one
'Til by fortune, Kulakoonstru
Came to The Bellicose Dragon
In it's crowded midst he soon knew
Here is where lies his destiny!
Setting out to seek adventure,
‘Cross a similar soul came he.
Spake the Awesome One: "Noble sir,
Join me upon this quest of mine!"
They soon became fast friends in arms,
Sharing bread, meat and much fine wine,
Pledging to keep each from all harms.
Gath’ring these brothers together,
They went to seek experience,
They went to seek golden treasure.
This has become the legend since.

Kulakoonstru! Kulakoonstru!
Diamond Wielder! Tech Wielder!
Ability Wielder! Lithon Wielder!
Supplier of Clarth's Petroni!
Close, Personal Friend of the Death God!
The Unseen! Time Traveler!
Shadow Walker! The Good!
Lord of Yaninas! LORD OF YANINAS!

II

Many hard fights they quickly found,
Many grievous wounds, many deaths.
Many quiet nights on cold ground
To think their companion’s last breaths.
Piles of treasure, gleaming and gold,
Sparkling gems and polished jewels,

Could not be found among the old
Bones of monsters slain in duels.
Treasure eluded the party,
Though they battled fearsome undead,
Lycanthropes, and they fought hardy.
In despair Kulakoonstru said:
"We must away to the far north,
Where the mountains jut from the land.
Only there may we prove our worth,
Vanquish rich monsters with bare hand!"
So went the group to the tall peaks,
Sharp swords, arrows nocked on the bow.
Days and nights made many long weeks.
At last one day the sun, sunk low,
Shone gilded mountains far away.
His Awesomenessness[5] said to them:
"Soon we will reach there, one more day,
Packs filled with treasure to the brim!"
So entered they that treacherous place,
Fanned out, eyes watchful all around.
Nay, they were not afraid to face
The fearsome creatures that they found.
Many difficult battles fought,
Many of the friends sadly died.
They found the treasures that they sought,
Near ev'ry monster a lair to hide.
O! But soon the party dwindled.
Till there was only one close friend.
Still within their hearts were kindled
Flames of adventure till the end!
Very slowly they were walking

[5] "Awesomenessness" is translated from the ancient Yanina as best as can be. It's meaning is something like: "the greatest of all time and everyone knows it". Clearly apt in this case.

Through the mountains' rough, rocky brush,
Quiet, stealthy hunters stalking
Loathsome creatures they would then crush,
Hearing clear a whistle's sound out
A far distance they were looking
Seeing what was without a doubt
A giant's fine entrance-making.
"Greetings!" did cry Kulakoonstru
"How fare you on this wondrous day?"
The giant said "Fine, whom are you?"
"A jolly party on our way
To venture for epic glory!"
The giant was called Clarth[6] and he
Told of his compelling story.
Then he bid them come with and see
Another place, another plane.
Lacking any close ties to here
They joined him then with joy unfeigned,
Without regrets, and without fear.

Kulakoonstru! Kulakoonstru!
Diamond Wielder! Tech Wielder!
Ability Wielder! Lithon Wielder!
Supplier of Clarth's Petroni!
Close, Personal Friend of the Death God!
The Unseen! Time Traveler!
Shadow Walker! The Good!
Lord of Yaninas! LORD OF YANINAS!

III

So off they set to travel planes,

---

[6] Clarth was a legendary True-Titan, his ultimate fate is unknown at this time.

Dimensions, times, universes.
Each one would Clarth with care explain,
In each would they fill their purses.
Kulakoonstru gained much great skill
With his awesome sword and longbow,
More cunning and swift was each kill.
Then they met a single man, lo!
He challenged them their right to pass.
Clarth then commenced to smite him dead,
The man displayed a power vast
That the True-Titan grimly said:
"I will now draw my brother's[7] sword
And you will surely then perish!"
Across a gulf of time so broad
Was pulled a weapon to cherish.
Gleaming in the day's bright sunlight,
A surfeit of diamond-forged strength.
Seeing this, the man blanched in fright,
And fled from the sword's glowing length.
They marveled at the sword's power,
Too soon must it go to the past,
For it was not this sword's hour;
That day will arrive much too fast.
On they went, much treasure taking.
They yearned not for the world behind
Legends they were in the making,
Legends in their very own time.
They went by a river flowing,
Who's current was like a great laugh.
Swiftly a squirrel was clawing
Gashes in Clarth's great bulging calf.

---

[7] Clarth's brother is even more obscure, very few references mention him, but he is presumably also a True Titan of significant power.

He killed it with a single blow,
He then fell in a deadly harm.
That it was cursed, he did not know.
So how to break this nightmare charm[8]?
Clarth tumbled down and shivering.
Exhausted eyes barely open,
His body fev'rish, aquiv'ring.
They looked on horror beyond ken.
Kulakoonstru cried, "We shall save
Our gallant giant friend lying
Here, or soon he'll be deep a' grave!"
With some beer for fortifying!
Then they commenced the summoning
Of worshipped beings. The Death God,
Goddess of Life[9], the all-seeing
Unknown God[10], who is a god's god.
They pleadingly called Clarth's brother
Who lay tortured in a dungeon.
They thought 'bout calling another;
The mighty God of Destruction[11].
When fair Goddess of Life, she came,
Clarth was in a dire descent.
When his kinfolk called out his name:
"O! Clarth, for you I do lament!
"But, these two gallant friends of yours
"Must save you, I can't do the deed!"

---

[8] Cursed squirrels are not unknown, even in our present time. As are ludicrous tiny ants that can kill with a single bite, or at least these ants have been rumored to exist somewhere.

[9] The Death God and the Goddess of Life were very ancient gods, they are no longer present in our existence. While they are not mythical, they have not been encountered for many millennia.

[10] This "Unknown God" is a reference to a being that has never been documented as existing. This may simply be an exaggeration of the author's.

[11] For the God of Destruction, cf. note 9.

Both cried: "Help this comrade of ours!"
Then Goddess replied, "Who we need
Is the Death God. I shall fetch him."
And swiftly she was gone away.
As Clarth's life flame was growing dim,
And Kulakoonstru begged him stay,
Goddess returned, shining glory,
Bringing the Red-Eyed deity.
God’s red eyes glowed at the story
Of Clarth's defeat and agony.
"This can’t be, he is a shaper
Of Multiverse's destiny!"
Death God’s magic commenced to cure,
"I must needs bring him back to thee!"
Goddess of Life lent her power.
And “poof”: the deadly curse was gone
And so Clarth was freed that hour.
They thanked the gods, the gods went on.
Clarth recovered and thanked the two,
Kulakoonstru and his comrade.
"I must give reward to those who
Saved my life from a squirr’l gone bad!
I shall grow your latent powers,
Both of you have powers in thee.
For helping me through dark hours,
I bring forth your ability!"
So upon that day was bestowed
The foremost awesome epithet,
The initial of massive loads,
The beginning of the vast set,
The titles of Kulakoonstru:
Lo! The Ability Wielder!
He is now a Yanina who
Can detect his foes anywhere!

Presently Clarth was of a mind
To take his leave of both the two.
Other gifts he would leave behind,
"Great power and gold to help you
Continue in these foul places!"
To each was presented a boon
To bring light to their glad faces.
Kulakoonstru was like to swoon
Over this generous token.
Here was an awesome black diamond.
Too glad for words to be spoken
He could barely say, "Thanks, my friend."
He added a new epithet,
A new regal title of worth,
Another for the growing set:
He was Diamond Wielder henceforth!
Yet even more was Clarth to give,
He shrank to a child's tiny size
Clarth made a means for them to live.
He grew again before their eyes,
And presented his masterpiece.
A golden sculpture of the two,
It's beauty could make one's heart cease[12].
Here was a valuable statue,
And upon return to their home
It could be reluctantly sold
To any prestigious person,
In exchange for huge sums of gold.
Clarth ported them to the city,
And bade them a fond fare thee well:
"Call upon me be you needy!
And I may visit where you dwell!"

---

[12] This statue has never been located, but it is clearly a priceless relic, and would be the centerpiece of any museum's collection.

Kulakoonstru! Kulakoonstru!
Diamond Wielder! Tech Wielder!
Ability Wielder! Lithon Wielder!
Supplier of Clarth's Petroni!
Close, Personal Friend of the Death God!
The Unseen! Time Traveler!
Shadow Walker! The Good!
Lord of Yaninas! LORD OF YANINAS!

IV

They went back, their adventure done,
And set out to sell the statue.
They soon found a wealthy patron
Who the fine sculpture's value.
He gave them great gems and much gold
Even still they felt strangely sad,
For though it was meant to be sold,
They'd regret losing what they had.
They moved to regal sumptuous halls
They soon were weary of the life.
They yearned for life beyond the walls,
They wanted the fray and the strife.
They raised a brave group of beings
Who'd enter the dungeon with them,
To get treasure and magic things.
Now did their adventure begin.
Only four or five days from home
A large, light, strange object was found.
'Twas a mana[13]-rich glowing dome,
A mysterious, magic mound.

---

[13] Mana was supposedly the source of magic in the ancient times, prior to the discovery and utilization of chi.

No one could fathom what to do,
All were wondering about it.
It fell to brave Kulakoonstru,
Who used his great, powerful wit.
His awesomenessness walked forward
And said to the pulsating light:
"I wish a Petroni[14] clad sword
To increase my awesome great might!"
Lo! His sword[15] was covered in black,
Blacker than the darkest dark night.
"All my foes would fear to attack,
And would flee me in trembling fright"
Kulakoonstru cried with such glee.
To the mound's now newly dimmed glow
All the rest gathered 'round to see
If their wishes it might bestow.
But far and away the best was
The awesome blade of Petroni.
He was up most the night because
He displayed it for all to see.
Onward they went to the dungeon
And soon reached it's secret dark door.
With Kulakoonstru in rank one
The party stepped on Elven floor.
Past loathsome undead did they fight.
Hacking, hewing with all their strength,
In the dim glow of Elven light.
Until finally they came at length
To the third level, down river.

---

[14] Petroni is a mythical metal, derived from equally mythical beetles (see note 24). This metal is said to have unusual and spectacular properties. As of this publication (2nd ed.), none has ever been found.

[15] It is thought that this sword was the traditional Yanina jagged curved blade, but it has never been located.

Wondrous rooms they soon came upon,
Much gold slain foes did deliver.
A bright pool of liquid Lithon[16]
All their swords they dipped hilt deep in
Coating them with Elven metal.
Swords and armor fortified. Then,
An old, blind elf at them did yell:
"You must leave immediately!"
Forcing them from the pool's close room
Though the aged elf could not see,
His aspect radiated doom.
E'en in retreat the Lord was now
Clad in lithon from head to toe.
Keeping him safe in any row,
All would fear the Yanina foe!
He now gained the awesome title
Lithon Wielder, Kulakoonstru!
But they did not sit there idle,
Back into the dungeon and through
The secret passages that led
To great marvels in other rooms.
Several times they battled undead,
And many members met their dooms.
But still they explored on and on,
And came to a cavernous hall,
Where rested a staff of lithon,
But that was not the end at all.
For on a pillar gleamed a gem:
Purple diamond with red spiral!
Desire was kindled in them,

---

[16] Lithon is another magical or semi-magical metal, but unlike Petroni, this metal is known and, while not common, it is found in places throughout the world. It is harder than steel and lighter than any other metal. It is typically not found in liquid form.

Their stepping in sounded the call,
And they were quickly surrounded.
They had to fight through the Thorn[17] horde
Which was poised to strike them all dead.
So, drawing his Petroni sword
Kulakoonstru killed them swiftly.
All about them scattered in fear
Of the terrible sight to see:
Through skulls the black metal would tear,
Destroying all who were around.
Inexorably driven back
Our heroes were forced to give ground,
Furiously though they would hack,
More foes would replace their fallen.
So they went down the corridor,
Fleeing to where they had not been.
They came to a closed and locked door.
Inside did heroes slowly creep,
Torches flaring in the deep dark.
The saw ashes piled in a heap,
Beneath a glowing lightning arc.
Brave was Awesome One's companion
He went to touch the magic bolt,
He was shocked and glowed like the sun,
He did not die from the huge jolt.
He found he had a new power,
And Kulakoonstru tried to see,
If in this auspicious hour,
He might gain this ability.
So to the bolt he touched his hand

---

[17] Thorns were a race of servants that were used by the Elves. They were known as fearsome warriors. See the chapters on elves and their servants in: The Non-Yanina Races, 4th Ed. By Rodularkosuu, University of Arqnasquirg Press, p115 - 305 (specifically p283ff).

And the fierce white lightning crackled,
Flowing in to his body, and
Through him magic lightning traveled.
Another had been added to
The long list of abilities
Of the Awesome Kulakoonstru.
His sword causes foes hearts to freeze,
Now he can do great harm to them
With just a single gentle touch.
All will now fear and respect him,
Or suffer for not doing such!
The party again moved onward,
Searching for any great treasure,
Warily walking, hand to sword,
But with Kulakoonstru, secure.
Into a room with many doors,
Each with a god's sacred symbol,
They walked across the room's smooth floor,
Each to their own god's small temple.
Inside the Death God's sacred room,
Kulakoonstru faced a great test,
Which could have been his certain doom,
Had he not been the very best.
For being such a great hero
He was given a wondrous prize,
A Petroni tipped black arrow[18].
Black glow glinted off his eight eyes
And Kulakoonstru then did know,
By the gift the Death God did send,
And his titles again did grow:

---

[18] A Petroni tipped arrow is among the legendary artifacts made from this metal. It supposedly caused instant true death in whatever it struck. Sadly, it could only be used once. As a mythical weapon it is very powerful and was reportedly granted as a boon by the God of Death.

The Death God's Close, Personal Friend!
Other gifts were also there won,
And so they were ready to leave,
Adventure in this dungeon done.
But soon they all had cause to grieve,
Kulakoonstru's friend of long days
Met a sad and grievous demise,
In one of the myriad ways,
Under the clear, cold azure skies.
So of the two Clarth's Companions.
The one left is Kulakoonstru.
To the memory of the fallen,
Kulakoonstru will e'er be true.

Kulakoonstru! Kulakoonstru!
Diamond Wielder! Tech Wielder!
Ability Wielder! Lithon Wielder!
Supplier of Clarth's Petroni!
Close, Personal Friend of the Death God!
The Unseen! Time Traveler!
Shadow Walker! The Good!
Lord of Yaninas! LORD OF YANINAS!

V

The trip back was quick and easy,
A swift teleport and then home.
The flat seemed cheerless and empty,
He lost the desire to roam.
He sat around with his new gold
And did not go out too often,
Regretting still that they had sold
The statue of Clarth's Companions.
But then he grew restless once more

And set out in search of new friends.
Ones who would come on his quest for
That utmost awesome of diamonds.
Out he went to the city's inns,
Where the souls of valor gather,
And to the dark seedy taverns,
These only the city's slime lure.
He came upon two for his band,
Who's thirst for adventure was new.
One was called just Mahatmas, and
A Luck God[19] priest who was Tsuru.
He found that they were much like him,
They wanted to gain wealth and fame.
They gathered a party to them
And went to glorify their name.
Kulakoonstru had decided,
To put off his quest till later.
So this eager party he led
Just went out for the adventure.
Out they went, out seeking glory.
Eager to go where none had been,
Back to that third lower storey
Of the mystic Elven dungeon.
They passed under that dark threshold,
Battling the evil undead guards.
In search of the vast boundless gold
That lay hidden in many hoards.
Through the countless hallways they went,
Into the hidden secret rooms.

---

[19] The Luck God was another of the ancient gods. It is said he was a humorless son of a bitch who delighted only in tormenting people, even his own worshippers. Reportedly, he was also insufferably smug. Not much else is known about this ancient evil god. Nearly all traces of his existence have mercifully been removed.

Many swords they nicked and they bent
Sending evil things to their dooms.
Behind a sealed chained portal,
They found a marvelous item.
A dull grey, round glowing opal
Whose power did now entrance them.
Quickly they set out to get it,
Knowing it would not be easy.
They created a magic pit
And placing it where the guard be,
He fell down into the abyss,
The party recovered the gem.
But in testing they were amiss,
And it's power killed two of them.
They saw it was too powerful,
For their small unrefinéd skill,
They went to the Death God's temple
With the gem their coffers did fill.
For the immortal god was glad
They had brought this opal to him.
He gave them things they wished they had,
Abilities, awesome items,
For his close friend Kulakoonstru,
He of course saved only the best.
His abilities grew by two,
As his gifts were above the rest.
The Awesome of Yanina Lords
Can see in the darkest of nights.
Plus, should he be assailed by hordes,
He can now teleport in flight.
Armèd with such awesome power,
Kulakoonstru's new decision:
The time would be now or never!
He would get that purple diamond.

So he made his ingenious plan,
Getting needed accessories,
To that magical room he ran,
Tuning his vast abilities.
He came to the cavernous room
To face the challenge of his life,
The wrong move would surely bring doom,
Even the right move would bring strife.
So, as prepared as he could be,
He was ready to take the gem.
With his awesome ability,
He quickly did teleport in.
His Lithon mailed fist grasped the stone:
The staff summoned its defender.
An Elven being, made of bone,
Who threw the staff at his armor.
The staff cleaved the Elven metal
Kulakoonstru was sliced in two.
Yet he was not cowed, not at all,
He was Awesome Kulakoonstru!
He was ready for such a thing
And he used his potent magic.
His strong regeneration ring
Saved him from a fate so tragic.
Other magics whisked him away,
Safely from the Elven dungeon.
Into the bright sun of the day,
Where he could assess his diamond.
As it was sparkling in the light,
It was of the best quality.
He knew it would add to his might,
Would add to his ability.
He tested this brand new diamond,
To see the magic of the thing.

Three semi-titans were summoned,
To do Kulakoonstru's bidding.
He commanded the titans three
To protect and to preserve him,
As he walked back to the city
Evaluating his new gem.
So then they proceeded onwards
Through the oft-deadly wilderness,
Protected by the titans' swords,
And Kulakoonstru's great prowess.
Other powers he discovered:
The diamond would drain energy,
From wounds he quickly recovered.
'nother Awesome Ability!
When he got to his demesnes
His escort vanished in the air.
And to all his stunned companions
He was now The Diamond Wielder!

Kulakoonstru! Kulakoonstru!
Diamond Wielder! Tech Wielder!
Ability Wielder! Lithon Wielder!
Supplier of Clarth's Petroni!
Close, Personal Friend of the Death God!
The Unseen! Time Traveler!
Shadow Walker! The Good!
Lord of Yaninas! LORD OF YANINAS!

VI

Now the awesome Kulakoonstru,
With his massive diamond power,
Led all his faithful friends out to
A marvelous new adventure.

They decided to go explore
The Dungeon of Technology[20],
Where they had never been before,
And what they now wanted to see.
Off they went, to the northern parts,
To find the mystical dungeon.
They all went with emboldened hearts,
Because Kulakoonstru led them.
Far into the dangerous north,
They adventured out from their home.
Gaining great treasures of great worth
Onward they continued to roam.
As the mountains neared, days grew cold,
They came upon a strange being.
Leathery skin made it look old,
'Twas a giant, shouting greetings.
This peculiar giant became
A close friend to Kulakoonstru
So he was prompted to exclaim:
"To the dungeon I go with you!"
They came to the dungeon portal
Which went deep in the rocky ground,
Very confident, one and all
As Kulakoonstru led them down.
Through the smooth strangely lit hallway,
Down towards the dungeon's large main door.
When out from a secret doorway
A soldier sprang on to the floor!
The giant quickly dispatched him
And took from him strange armament.
They continued through the door, and
Down the curious halls they went.

---

[20] The Dungeon of Technology is known by another name: The Domain of Ron Sarn.

Corridors were strangely glowing,
With a peculiar luminance,
Every step, their caution growing,
With this novel experience.
They came on an ominous sight,
Faint lines of power could be seen
In the pale unnatural light,
Covering a peril unseen.
As they tested the fearsome pit
Their wooden spears were cut in two,
So they cautiously went to it
In looked Awesome Kulakoonstru.
He saw the shimmer of stasis.
Lithely leaping the deadly trap,
He turned and called to all the rest,
And adding the pit to their map.
They continued upon their way,
Encountering frequent patrols.
These were killed with alacrity.
They came to golden cloth in rolls.
Incautious Tsuru took a bolt,
Secreting it in his back pack.
Soon they reached an awesome threshold.
The two great metal doors swung back.
The dungeon lord then surveyed them,
Looking stern on his great high throne:
"You Yanina, have a strange gem!"
"Yes, sir, through much pain was it won!"
Said the Yanina back to him.
"And you, priest, were you planning to
"Abscond with that cloth you've hidden?"
Speechlessness of fear struck Tsuru.
The doors ominously slammed closed.
The party was now trapped within,

All surrounded by armored foes,
Who obeyed their master's dark whims.
As they struggled out of the room,
Bargaining many things away,
And all were saved from certain doom
As Kulakoonstru saved the day.
The Tech lord turned a greedy eye
Upon the crimson-purple stone.
"All in the chamber will now die,
"If this gem is not soon my own!"
So his Awesomenessness proposed
A trade to benefit all 'round.
The deal was very swiftly closed
The party was moved above ground.
Although the great diamond was lost,
Kulakoonstru was not upset.
True, it was a staggering cost,
But he had what he came to get.
He had the awesome flaming gun,
Which burns with the black diamond blaze.
But also did the lordly one
Have the marvelous stasis blade.
The great Yanina warrior
Adds 'nother title to his tales.
He now becomes the Tech Wielder!
"He is awesome!" everyone hails.

Kulakoonstru! Kulakoonstru!
Diamond Wielder! Tech Wielder!
Ability Wielder! Lithon Wielder!
Supplier of Clarth's Petroni!
Close, Personal Friend of the Death God!
The Unseen! Time Traveler!
Shadow Walker! The Good!

Lord of Yaninas! LORD OF YANINAS!

VII

A considerable portion of this canto survives intact. The initial few lines seem to be missing however. It is unclear what the "tragic day" at the beginning was referring to.

{missing} ...
... was a tragic day.
Yet still the band continued on.
Lairs they found, and lairs they raided.
Lo! Appeared one foul and profane!
This creature stood tall and stated:
"Puny beings, all must leave this plane!
"I will destroy you and others!
"This is not the place to be in!
"It is for me and my brothers!"
For this was, The Asshole Demon[21]!!

---

[21] The etymology of the name "Asshole Demon" is such that it is a literal translation of a proper name in the ancient demon tongue: "Be Na Tarth". The root "-tarth", generally means "demon", but it is typically used to specify only a male demon. And "be na" is understood to mean "asshole" in almost every language in existence, both modern and ancient. It is unclear why such universal agreement on a linguistic term should be, but the conjecture is that the being Be Na Tarth influenced the actual development of languages on multiple planes of existence, throughout all of history. Whether "Be Na" came first or his appellation as "Asshole" is a result of his name and character, is unknown at this time. In any case, "be na" is now understood to mean "asshole" by virtually everyone in all of recorded history. And in general, the abbreviated form of the name, simply "Asshole" (or more properly: "The Asshole Demon"), is universally known to identify Be Na Tarth.

N.B. Be Na Tarth, The Asshole Demon, was well known to our great god Silanarë. This demon's ignominious defeat is the

Kulakoonstru and the rest were
Shocked and appalled that The Asshole,
That most notorious monster,
That vile creature without a soul,
Would maliciously target all.
They tried to teleport away,
The Asshole prevented withdrawal.
He exclaimed with glee: "Not today!"
Then The Asshole began the rout,
As Kulakoonstru did succumb,
He sent one lone distressed plea out:
"Clarth, help, we cannot win this one!"
The True-Titan did hear the call,
He stretched forth his prodigious might
And snatched Kulakoonstru, and all!
Taking them from The Asshole's sight.
Incensed, The Asshole searched for them,
But his scouring was all for naught.
They were on a new dimension,
So that they could not now be caught.
Clarth spoke to his Yanina friend:
"'Twas my pleasure to remove your
"Party from the grasp of that fiend".
They returned near the dungeon's door.
The forest thickened around them,
The path became more treacherous.
Then they reached the Elven dungeon,
Treasure for the adventurous!

---

impetus for the Annual Festival of Justice, when the temples of Silanarë, Tenebrous and Fylgjukona all join together to grab their crotches and cry out the ritual exclamation of: "Smoke This, Laddie". It is still one of the holiest days in all of the universe. The fact that Kulakoonstru was also plagued by this foul creature (apparently more than once) is one of the more amazing links between his ancient time and our modern existence.

Deep into the myriad halls,
The company went down and down.
Through doors and even through the walls!
Further and further underground.
Around corners, down corridors,
Past a simple wall that looked plain,
But concealing a secret door!
Inside, a poor soul in great pain.
It looked to be a small dragon,
Held by outstretched wings to the wall
By cruel spikes made of lithon.
A sad creature, with a sad call.
Kulakoonstru became enraged
That such a fine, majestic being,
Would be foully tortured and caged.
"Oh no! I will set to freeing
"This poor wretch, who is so abused."
Tech Wielder then brought out his blade
Of stasis from Ron Sarn[22], and used
It on the spikes, but was dismayed!
The Lithon was just barely scratched.
Kulakoonstru said to all 'round:
"I will never be overmatched!
Ere long it be, I'll get him down!"
With a nip from his whisky flask,
Kulakoonstru commenced his deed,
His famed effort, his storied task,
With much sweat the dragon was freed.
Restored, it thanked Kulakoonstru:
"O Great one, many thanks," he said
"I'm forever obliged to you."
Kulakoonstru heard in his head.

---

[22] Cf. Canto VI, note 19.

The dragon nods and does then leave,
The party is awed and amazed,
A great deed was done, all believe.
Proceeding through halls like a maze.
Down a short passage to a door,
Listen warily and enter.
And see some Petroni armor!
'Twas in the room's very center,
It somehow seemed slightly tainted.
Brave Kulakoonstru picked it up,
Sadly he instantly fainted,
He started dying; his backup
Magic items[23] brought him back to
The temple of the God of Death.
The god was summoned and he knew
He must restore his Close Friend's breath.
And so the great Death God labored,
To bring life back to his close friend,
And lo! Kulakoonstru was cured,
Ready to return and contend
With this cursed Petroni treasure.
"Underworld Lord 'twas the charmer",
Spoke the Death God, of the measure
Cursing the black suit of armor.
"Take care if you mean to snatch it.
"Do not bring here unpurified.
"This I will not ever permit.
"True Flame makes the curse nullified."
Kulakoonstru needed a plan
To get and ameliorate

[23] It is thought that this is in reference to the one or more special magic items that Kulakoonstru had that would return him to the Death God temple should bad occurrences befall him, as they often did.

The deadly evil infection.
He needs a horizontal gate!
Slide the gate 'neath the Petroni,
And drop it in the sky outside,
Where his dragon friend would there be,
To burn the fetid curse aside.
This brilliant plan could now not fail.
And so Kulakoonstru did call
His friend, and he did sent the mail
Outside into the sky to fall.
At his behest the dragon came
And did as Kulakoonstru asked.
Bathed the cursed armor in True Flame,
A prodigious, great mile long blast!
The Petroni suit was destroyed,
Which all had said impossible!
Kulakoonstru was thus annoyed,
This outcome was unusual.
How did True Flame burn Petroni?
Even the flames from a dragon?
All scholars say it could not be,
That such a thing should not happen![24]
His friend, the dragon-like creature,
Is one of a kind and special!
They went again to adventure
Back home, and ever so careful.
Turned from the mountains and went south,

[24] All the scant available research on the legendary Petroni bears this assertion out. Nowhere is it said that Petroni can even be pierced, much less destroyed. Even by True Flame. Clearly, this "dragon" friend of Kulakoonstru's is more than a regular dragon. Also, no known dragon could produce a "mile long blast" of True Flame, and even assuming the description is an exaggeration, even one-third of it would be more True Flame than the most powerful dragon ever known would breathe.

Taking the long adventure home.
Leaving behind the deadly north.
On the long way back they spied some
Glowing black shelled giant beetles;
They had Petroni carapace![25]
Kulakoonstru was then gleeful,
He vowed to instantly replace
The Petroni that was consumed.
He'd call, Clarth who'd be astounded
He knew the Titan's gratitude
For this prize would be unbounded.
The True Titan is able to
Take the raw element and shape
Things, and this Kulakoonstru knew.
With this, who knows what he would make?
Kulakoonstru bound the black horde,
And killed them by putting the prized,
Awesome Petroni coated sword,[26]
Into their vulnerable eyes.
It was the only way to slay
These impenetrable vermin.
Now all Kulakoonstru needs say:
"Clarth, come to me, my great, great friend!"
Clarth came to them and looked around
And he was thoroughly amazed
By what he saw dead on the ground.
Kulakoonstru he greatly praised.
"O! Great Yanina companion,
"I must thank thee for this", said he.
"And now a new designation:

---

[25] This may be the source of Petroni itself, though no other independent confirmation exists. These "Petroni beetles" have never been recorded elsewhere and are certainly no longer in existence today.

[26] See Canto IV.

"Supplier of Clarth's Petroni!"

Kulakoonstru! Kulakoonstru!
Diamond Wielder! Tech Wielder!
Ability Wielder! Lithon Wielder!
Supplier of Clarth's Petroni!
Close, Personal Friend of the Death God!
The Unseen! Time Traveler!
Shadow Walker! The Good!
Lord of Yaninas! LORD OF YANINAS!

VIII

There are fragments of this particular canto that survive. It begins with what seems to be a trip to Slar Mar[27]. It is there where Kulakoonstru met the Zintu[28] for the first time. However, the only surviving passages of the canto refer to Kulakoonstru's group going to a currently undocumented dungeon, presumably on the way back from Slar Mar:

{missing}...
As the last rays of sun were seen,
Kulakoonstru led his group on
To Arkoth[29] where no one had been,
Seeking wealth they may come upon.
They moved through the long corridors,
To where they could just barely see.

---

[27] "Slar Mar" - The Desert of Death. Don't go there.

[28] "Zintu are feline looking bi-peds. They are covered in fur and have retractable claws." The Non-Yanina Races, 4th Ed. By Rodularkosuu, University of Arqnasquirg Press, see p331 - 344 for more details.

[29] Very little is known about the referenced Arkoth. Is it a place, as described here, or is Arkoth actually a being as referenced later in the text? Further research clearly needs to be undertaken.

The wizards and the warriors,
Searching the dungeon for booty.
Down the long cold, dark passageway
They came to a flashing white rune,
Above a pit at a four-way:
"Jump for a quest and a great boon!"
To astute folk, this seemed a trap.
Kulakoonstru was not foolish,
He added this bait to his map.
"Who would fall for...
...{missing}

Much of the text from this point is either missing or unreadable. I am unsure how extensive the gap is. The text again becomes legible near the very end of the canto.

{missing} ...
... proceeded to the end,
A grumpy wastrel was about.
He threatened to leave them all dead.
Tsuru spoke and did weakly shout:
"My God will come and have your head!"
He chortled with undisguised mirth:
"You? A lowly priest, not so high?
"If be you so great, bring him forth!"
With no choice, but to try or die,
He stammered: "I shall summon him!"
The man grinned and the battle loomed.
Sweating, Tsuru waved his hands then,
Though it appeared that all were doomed,
When the fiend started to attack,
A very strange rumbling was heard.
The dungeon walls began to crack,
Absurdly, the Luck God appeared!

"Tsuru, my great friend, how are you?
"What have you been doing lately?
"I see you've brought Kulakoonstru!"
The god turned to the enemy.
"It is your unlucky day, sir.
"For menacing thus my good friend.
"Strange, unexpected things occur."
Suddenly the ceiling caved in,
Squashing the stunned hapless foe dead.
As the dust settled, Tsuru bowed,
The rest rolled their eyes in their head.
"Too bad, so sad," the Luck God crowed.
Waving to all he disappeared
Into the dust swirling about.
Kulakoonstru sighed as it cleared
"I have had enough of that lout
"To last many a century!"
Tsuru bristled...
...{missing}

There is no more extant text for this canto.

IX

This canto is from a missing scroll. But based on several other sources, and the timeline associated with the prior and subsequent cantos, I infer that this canto dealt primarily with some of Clarth's and Kulakoonstru's newer adventures. It is suggested that Kulakoonstru was given some kind of magical item, a card of some kind, that he could use to contact Clarth, no matter where either of them might be. And even more astounding they could travel to each other through this card. It is an amazing artifact if it truly existed.

X

There are only a few fragments of this canto. Most deal with a battle Kulakoonstru et. al. had involving a party of Surgarun. The Surgarun are and were nominally neutral to Yaninas, but as he was accompanied by several humans, including the apparently male Tsuru, they attacked without warning. The battle is in progress as the fragment commences. Soon, the Queen[30] of the Surgarun appeared. Things rapidly escalated from there as can be seen in the text.

{missing} ...
...wielding tech
Against treacherous Surgarun!
Their sad, weak ranks he then did wreck!
To their weak strikes he was immune!
Desperately, frantically they called
Out to be rescued by their queen.
When she came, all were so appalled!
Ne'er was such malevolence seen.
Tsuru ran back to his temple,
For the capricious God of Luck.
Kulakoonstru was more careful.
Exclaiming: "What the fucking fuck?"
The queen, cut an evil figure,
Turned to the Yanina and said:
"You'll pay for slaying my sisters!"
He feared he would quickly be dead.
With teleport ability,
He went to meet up with Tsuru,
At Luck God's shrine in the city,

[30] This would have been before the Queen of the Surgarun, Sharalaca, was raised to goddesshood and became a friend and ally of our great god Silanarë.

Mahatmas did flee to there too.
The queen followed to the temple!
Priests were agog in abject fright.
Forces began to assemble:
The Luck God came, ready to fight.
Kulakoonstru called Clarth, else die.
He reached out to his dragon friend,
Who appeared in the clear blue sky.
The people thought it was the end!
The Surgarun queen was enraged:
The party dared defend itself!
The Death God had to be engaged:
"Sharalaca, this won't end well;
"Assaulting my Personal Friend."
Miles of flame came from the dragon.
Clarth drew his prismatic sword and
Looked sternly at the Surgarun.
The Luck God was flipping a coin,
Muttering to himself dismally.
The City's General then did join
And did say loudly, angrily:
"All right, all right, what's all this then?
"Is this the Queen of Surgarun?
"What is that strange looking dragon?
"And," he gaped at the True-Titan.
"Oh shit," he said and stopped talking.
The Death God strode into the midst,
"Sharalaca, stop your stalking
"Of my close friend and all the rest,
"We could all go our own ways then."
The queen fumed, but finally agreed.
"Do not let me see him again!"
She went back to her lands with speed.
The General saw Kulakoonstru:

"Though you have a truce, understand,
"With the Surgarun, but from here you
"Will be forthwith for ten years, banned!"
A gasp went up, but he just smiled:
"I'll return greater than I was!
"Ten years will seem a small, short while."
He saluted to great applause!
Kulakoonstru and Clarth nod to
The Death God, and then vanishéd,
Joined by Mahatmas and Tsuru.
...{missing}

XI

In this existing fragment from the end of Canto XI, there is a description of a great festival or celebration that Kulakoonstru put on to commemorate his reaching a milestone in his life. I'm unsure of the milestone, but it appears to be associated with him gaining considerable prowess with his weapons and becoming an even more formidable warrior. Today warriors sometimes celebrate milestones such as this when they get promoted in rank or simply become more important. In Kulakoonstru's case, many of his friends came to this celebration.

It is probable that the celebration was in Arqnasquirg, since Kulakoonstru had been banned from Old Arbeneth just recently, also since it is mentioned that several Ssrýll attended, and they have never been welcome in the human cities. I know it was important because some of the finest legendary Yanina whiskies are mentioned as being served in some of the verses (see note 30).

{missing} ...an incredible
Fete for his rise in power!

All the best folk were plentiful!
They were the finest of the hour!
Clarth, legendary True-Titan.
Leathery Giant did attend.
There was a human named Vramin.
The Death God, his Personal Friend.
The one known only as Wesass.
The hapless Luck God priest Tsuru.
The human wizard Mahatmas.
And very important Ssrýll too.
There was beer from across the lands,
The tastiest brews known to be,
From brew master's delicate hands.
All there were so amazed to try
Such a vast selection of beer!
All there were moved to then cry:
"These special brews from far and near
"Assembled for us to all try!"
Beer there was from the mountain towns,
Beer from near to the salty sea.
Kegs were brought from upland and down
To slake the needs of the thirsty.
There was beer flowing from the taps,
And there was beer bottles clinking.
Mugs were raised high and hands did clap,
All did enjoy merry drinking!
They had beers from so far away,
Even Yaninas did not know!
The bar had such a vast array
That there was none that could say no.
Ale was had, from Old Arberneth,
Stout, brewed by Clarth was also there.
Pilsners that takes away one's breath,
Lagers were found among the fare.

Rare moon beer from another plane
Was brought there by a friend so true,
It tasted like a new spring rain,
'Twas special to Kulakoonstru.
The Death God brought a malty Bock
That fast went to everyone's head.
To this brew everyone did flock,
As it truly could raise the dead!
Even more tasty brews were seen,
Some had never been served before.
The Ssrýll brought one that looked as green,
But turned to dark upon the pour.
The Leathery Giant did bring
A pale brew for all to imbibe.
It was near clear as pure spring,
That no one could really describe.
Even Tsuru brought forth a brew.
From the Luck God temple in town.
It was cloudy, hard to see through,
And was difficult to keep down.
Friends from near and from far brought forth.
So many delectable beers,
From the east, south, west and the north,
All were greeted with hearty cheers!
The beer flowed many happy days,
The guests partook as they so willed.
Kulakoonstru showed all the ways
That empty beer mugs could be filled!
The long weeks of celebration,
Leading to the final hours,
Where there would be adulation
And the triumph of his powers.
This great celebration would end
With the ultimate festival.

Squirg for all who thus did attend.
Squirg that was most commendable!
It came from the misty lowlands.
It came from in the green valleys.
It came from the cold, cold highlands.
From the finest malted barleys.
All was exquisite perfection!
All was the finest that e'er been.
The best for the celebration!
The squirg was the rarest e'er seen!
There was Pholis from the islands,
Many casks of rare Biroray.
Ancient Old Flen from the highlands.
All were amazed by the array!
Squirg was had that was all so rare
'Twas not been tasted in decades.
There were barrels of the best fare,
Including several of Tranade.
Ugurulin poured in fair glass,
Made for many Yanina toast!
Peaty and strong, with hints of grass,
All who imbibed could brashly boast:
"Ho yay! Kulakoonstru the great!
"Ho yay! You are the special one!
"Ho yay! All your squirg is first rate!
"Ho yay! To the victories you've won!"
Many brought with them single malts
To bestow on Kulakoonstru.
In these none could find any faults,
These were all like the finest dew
Others brought some distinguished blends,
Made from the rarest of the rare.
His many close, personal friends
Brought squirg so remarkably fair.

Dusty bottles of Horenur
Graced the long tables of the guests.
All could enjoy the malt so pure,
As all shared in the very best.
Fine decanters of Stagamore,
Some of the oldest squirg e'er known!
Woody tasting, like squirg of yore!
The heat warms one to the bone.
Many bottles of the Ardglee
Were also brought from peaty swamps.
These increased all the revelry,
Loud were the shouts, loud were the stomps!
This was a momentous event,
All of import did seek entry.
A vast fortune was wisely spent
On the bash of the century.
Only the finest, best vintage,
Would do for this awesome party.
One hundred year old Fulirdrage,
Casks of Maclenuru[31] whisky!
Everyone there, their glasses raised,
To toast his skill and gravitas.
From all was Kulakoonstru praised!
The greatest of all Yaninas!

Kulakoonstru! Kulakoonstru!

---

[31] Maclenuru is, perhaps, the most famous Yanina squirg (whisky) ever to be distilled. It is known to have been coveted by the gods themselves! See Maclenuru: Myth or Real?, By Fikurnoalin, Institute For Squirg Studies, p2-32. The fact that Kulakoonstru was able to secure several casks of this squirg for his celebration is beyond remarkable. No one, in all of Yanina history, has ever reported having more than a tiny flask of Maclenuru. This is conceivably Kulakoonstru's single greatest achievement. It certainly makes every Yanina in existence jealous of him and of this celebration.

Diamond Wielder! Tech Wielder!
Ability Wielder! Lithon Wielder!
Supplier of Clarth's Petroni!
Close, Personal Friend of the Death God!
The Unseen! Time Traveler!
Shadow Walker! The Good!
Lord of Yaninas! LORD OF YANINAS!

XII

This canto is, sadly, completely missing. In fact, there is no extant information about Kulakoonstru during the timeframe that this canto would be expected to cover, right after his celebration referenced in Canto XI to the events in Canto XIII. We do know that various unknown events must have occurred because the next canto has a number one more than would be the case if there were nothing between them. This is an unfortunate loss to the scholarship of Kulakoonstru.

XIII

There is quite a bit happening in this fragment from Canto XIII. There's some tragedy, and some very brilliant tactical moves by Kulakoonstru chronicled. Also the party goes to the Demon Dungeon[32].

{missing} ... lithon return arrow[33],

---

[32] The Demon Dungeon is also known as "Sar Tarth De-Mar" and is a notoriously dangerous place. It is remarkable that Kulakoonstru is known to have ventured in there multiple times and survived.

[33] I believe this is an arrow, that when shot at a target will poison the victim with a (nearly always) fatal poison and then magically return to the archer. It is believed to move faster than a normal arrow and being lithon tipped, it will penetrate virtually all known armor.

As he is the Lithon Wielder[34]!
And is now a greater hero!
They went to the Elven dungeon.
In to a small room Tsuru rushed,
Unknown animals were summoned.
By ten elephants, he was crushed!
Here in this place, his luck ran out.
Kulakoonstru wept, lamented:
"He was a good friend; true and stout!
"And here doth his story ended!"
The sad group started towards their home.
Soon they were viscously attacked
By a band of Hlats[35] on the roam.
Deadly fell foes, with fur of black!
They came in waves from the clear sky,
Relentless, and psychic powered.
Shaped like humans, but they could fly,
They attacked as they came downward.
The party did try to react,
Shooting bolts and magical spells.
Foul Hlats avoided all contact,
Nothing would e'er be their death knell!
The Hlats psychically evaded,
Nothing they could do would hurt them!
No one could fight these unaided,
So the group retreated in shame.
Kulakoonstru became enraged,
Shouting angrily of: "The Plan!!"
So, many scholars were engaged,
To defeat the Hlats, if they can!

---

[34] See Canto IV.

[35] For more information on Hlats, again see: The Non-Yanina Races, 4th Ed. By Rodularkosuu, University of Arqnasquirg Press, p312 - 330.

The human lore masters report:
"They can teleport psychically
"You must then block this teleport
"For your victory, this is key."
They sought out an item that could
Block the Hlats psychic escape route.
And damn the cost, this item should
Allow the Hlats to be wiped out!
The aggrieved adventurers stalked
Those foul Hlats, tracking to their lair.
And with their new item, they blocked
The creatures' escape in thin air!
The Hlats unable to take flight,
Their psychic wings were thusly clipped,
They had to stay and fairly fight.
The Hlats prepared to be now whipped!
The battle was waged endlessly,
Yet the party showed their toughness,
In defeating this enemy.
There were modicums justice.
...{missing}

It appears that other parts of this canto are also missing, since the scroll breaks off here and continues in a different part, at the start of a new adventure. The two sections of the physical scroll do not fit together at this point, and it is unclear how much is missing from the text. I think that both fragments belong to the same canto (XIII) because the previous and subsequent canto headings are extant.

{missing} ...
Mahatmas and Kulakoonstru
Went off to the Demon Dungeon.
A deadly place they'd not been to.

On the way, gold! glory! was won.
They arrived and found a warning.
It said: "No Entrance" but they scoffed!
They saw a western door burning,
Infernos did not scare them off!
They ventured west and then turned left,
And quickly it grew much hotter!
Heat ahead caused them much distress,
Such heat was not quenched by water.
Back to the northern passageway
They went down the east corridor,
Walking, wary for all foul play,
Followed it 'til they reached a door.
They could hear screams of agony.
The door was locked, but they forced it.
They slowly entered and did see:
A chained demoness, being whipped!
There was a black, floating whip and
A giant head of The Asshole
Staring at someone with tied hands.
Screaming, it was taking a toll.
Her eyes opened and she saw them,
A pleading look came to her mien.
The rescuers sprang to action,
And they cut through the Lithon chains.
She slumped to the ground, like a doll.
But quickly awoke, her eyes wide:
"Run, ere arrival of Asshole!"
Her weak powers moved them outside.
She recovered, she got stronger,
And moved them to a place afar.
Bowing, a captive no longer.

"I am known as: Slin Rac An Mar.[36]
"I was chained by Asshole Demon."
Kulakoonstru grimaced and sighed.
"Ah, I see that you have met him?"
"Indeed, 'twas nasty. I survived."
Said she: "Asshole put me in chains,
"To be given endless torment.
"Never to be free from that pain.
"Thank you for making it relent."
Slin Rac An Mar pledged loyalty
To the two brave adventurers.
"Call whenever you may need me,
"I will come, in or out of doors!"
Kulakoonstru bowed, best he could,
And spoke words of friendship to her:
"It is our great honor, we would
...{missing}

XIV

Canto XIV is mostly missing as well. But an early fragment is present, with the canto header. It seems to have begun as an adventure with Mahatmas to and in Arkoth. A large section of the body is then missing. The text resumes with a battle with some kind of ram creature, possibly named Glonteir. Kulakoonstru acquired a ring of invisibility and consequently, added another new title: "The Unseen"[37].

And once again they journeyed forth,

---

[36] Slin Rac An-Mar is a well known powerful demoness, and a nemesis of The Asshole Demon (see note 20). So she is obviously an ally of all good folk. There exists an archaic spelling seen in some sources of: Slin Rok An-Mar.

[37] See the appendix for a complete list of Kulakoonstru's known titles.

To add to the fabled story!
Off they ventured, off to Arkoth,
Seeking treasures and great glory.
They found the...

...{missing}...
...battle did commence.
Down another long dark hallway,
They began to enter a room,
Glonteir the ram stood; barred the way.
The pair then fought to overcome
The horned menace who sought conflict.
It was defeated, by skills great.
Many great wounds they did inflict,
And sent the goat to his dark fate!
A magic ring was found to gleam,
It rendered one invisible!
Kulakoonstru was The Unseen!
Thus added another title.

Kulakoonstru! Kulakoonstru!
Diamond Wielder! Tech Wielder!
Ability Wielder! Lithon Wielder!
Supplier of Clarth's Petroni!
Close, Personal Friend of the Death God!
The Unseen! Time Traveler!
Shadow Walker! The Good!
Lord of Yaninas! LORD OF YANINAS!

XV

This canto is another that is almost entirely missing from the scrolls. The final few stanzas are extant and tell the tale of how Kulakoonstru was somehow thrust very far back in time, and had to make his way back to his present day. It also briefly describes the creation and function of the magical statue that was found in the cask along with the scrolls and the cylinder seal.

{missing} ...
And passed through a temporal gate,
"Where have I been transported to?"
What now, is Kulakoonstru's fate?
He tried to call Clarth, the Titan,
No help came to get homeward bound.
Next was his Close, Personal Friend,
The Death God, but he was not found.
And the Unknown God[38] did not come!
Kulakoonstru remained steadfast.
No civilization begun,
These many epochs in the past.
That the future knew his story,
He carved his tale in stone tablets,
To leave them for all history.
Every place he went, these he left.[39]
Kulakoonstru was wandering from
The blue sea to the wild mountains.
To despair he would not succumb.
Miles numbered in the thousands.
Only the beasts and birds were there,
No elves, not even the Blo-een[40].

---

[38] See Canto III, note 10.

[39] Sadly, none of these precious artifacts have ever been located. It is believed that Kulakoonstru was over 3 million years in the past, so this is not unexpected.

[40] The Blo-een are thought to be one of the original races that came to this plane, or possibly initially existed here. They numbered in great hordes and would attack by spewing foam to immobilize their enemies. No Blo-een have been seen for many thousands of years, it is thought that they are extinct. The Non-

He did roam, here and everywhere,
Not a single being was seen.
As he roamed, the Death God appeared,
"Close, Personal Friend, I've found you!
"When you vanished, the worst was feared,
"A mighty effort did ensue!
"We finally found you in the past,
"Such a hurdle did not deter
"All from getting you at long last!
"You will now be Time Traveler!"
To show his thanks, Kulakoonstru
Gave the temple, to their delight,
A great Kulakoonstru statue
That will gloriously recite:

Kulakoonstru! Kulakoonstru!
Diamond Wielder! Tech Wielder!
Ability Wielder! Lithon Wielder!
Supplier of Clarth's Petroni!
Close, Personal Friend of the Death God!
The Unseen! Time Traveler!
Shadow Walker! The Good!
Lord of Yaninas! LORD OF YANINAS!

XVI

The Awesome Lord of Yaninas
Decided he must have a task.
With the wizard Mahatmas,
He went off to Arkoth to ask.
There they jumped down in the deep pit,
And came out visiting a man,

Yanina Races, 4th Ed. By Rodularkosuu, University of Arqnasquirg Press, p24 - 60.

Who requested that they please sit.
And magically waving his hand
He caused refreshments to appear,
Delicacies from 'round the world;
Including smooth Yanina beer.
They partook as their task unfurled.
"You must needs go to a far land,
"To take from a barbarous king
"A deadly box of power, and
"To Arkoth this box you shall bring!
You will get an awesome reward".
They agreed to perform the task.
And to the quest they went onward,
Though there were still questions to ask.
Off to lands of Alin Aru[41],
Went the brave human Mahatmas.
To see Clarth went Kulakoonstru,
To get his wisdom for the cause.
Armed with new knowledge of the foe,
Who's island they must now invade,
With Clarth's timely assist to go
To the island, their way they made.
Lost, without a clue of the way
The two walked towards the warm, white sand,
They espied a secluded bay,
Starting to walk 'round the island.
After several days of walking
They saw a leathery giant.
Kulakoonstru began talking
And he found him quite compliant.

---

[41] The Alin Aru are a well known sea-faring race. They have ranged all over the world's oceans. ibid., p75 - 91. Mahatmas no doubt consulted them for information on how to get to the unknown location specified by the quest giver.

The giant told of the city
Where was the ruler of the land,
He told them they were unfriendly
With those who came to the island.
Still, the two gallant companions
Proceeded to investigate.
So, to the new destination
They went with all stealth and all haste.
As the neared the small coastal town
They found themselves soon surrounded.
To the king they were taken down,
Who's mercy was not unbounded.
He forced them out of his kingdom,
Without so much as a kind word.
They returned whence they had come from,
Lacking their quest's final reward.
They must be subtle in the quest,
To get this strange, mystical box.
They must get advice from the best,
And be more clever than a fox.
They sought help from the True-Titan,
Who's wisdom is known epoch-wide,
Who's lore surpasses any man,
And is on Kulakoonstru's side.
Clarth spake to them much sage wisdom,
But he then gave them even more!
A magical yellow diamond,
To be used as a Shadow-door.
Thus, the noble Kulakoonstru
Adds another appellation
To many wonders he can do,
Shadow Walker, The Awesome One!
With this magic now in their hand,
They embark once more on the quest.

They shadow walk to the island,
And they attempt to do their best.
In the shadows they then approach,
And espying the hiding place,
Through the darkness they do encroach,
With that classic Yanina grace.
In haste they enter the small room
And they see the box' warden,
They prepare to bring it swift doom,
This very powerful demon.
Tech Wielder bares his laser sword,
Set to cleave the demon in twain.
Kulakoonstru swings, a hit scored!
The demon's curse is now his bane!
With a spectacular blue spark,
The laser sword is then damaged,
Yet the foul demon has no mark!
They leave fast as can be managed.
Demon lore they must needs now find,
To learn more of this evil foe.
So that into dust they may grind,
This cursed cause of all their woe.
Slin Rac An Mar herself them told,
How the demon was thusly bound.
By mighty spells from days of old,
With awesome power most profound:
"A mere dagger must slay this guard,
"No other weapon may harm it.
"With nothing else will it be marred,
"While upon the chair it doth sit."
The quest did now seemed nigh hopeless;
As they pondered the dreary plight.
Yet with new found bravery boundless,
They vowed to continue the fight.

At great pain and at huge expense,
Surely they must now arm themselves,
For both attack and for defense.
Into their meager funds they delve.
As unto paupers they become,
But with the proper tools at hand,
And plans to kill the foul demon,
They go again to the island.
The Petroni death-dagger[42] to
Defeat the black hellspawn demon.
The diamond that will protect you[43]
From all horrible damage done.
The gallant two again go forth,
To fulfill the quest as given.
Again will they prove their great worth,
The demonic head be riven!
They travel to the island realm.
With the shadow attack surprise
The enemy they will o'erwhelm.
The assault they again reprise.
Emerging ready for a fight.
Wielding the Petroni dagger,
Mahatmas shows his fearsome might,
He becomes the new attacker!
Kulakoonstru pulls the treasure
Into the dark, shadowy land,
Then the vile king doth did ensure

---

42 It is rumored that the if the legendary Petroni is forged in to a dagger, it will cause true-death in whomever is struck by it. Clearly, that was the plan envisioned here. It is unclear how they acquired one.

43 This is obviously a reference to a diamond with the power colloquially known as "Ultra-Protection". These diamonds are not easy to come by, and this may be the explanation for the references a few lines prior where the adventurers became "paupers" in the securing of one.

A battle to be fought by hand.
He must possess the magic throne,
Kulakoonstru must now win out
He must take the chair for his own
To return with victory to tout.
As the great Awesome one struggles
With his dark malevolent foe,
His valiant effort redoubles
To force the king to let it go.
Mahatmas grapples his rival.
One stab of the Petroni knife,
The demon fights for survival,
He sees the near end of his life.
But the foul beast will not just fall.
He assaults Mahatmas again,
Trying to bring him back to hell.
He does not want to be taken
So he calls the equine shadow
To deal with this foul, vile hell-spawn.
Black[44] brings his full fury on to
This demon and then sends him down
To the true-death he was so due.
Mahatmas does indeed survive,
Besting the demon, he withdrew,

[44] This is maddeningly obscure. "Equine shadow" (or "shadow equine", but that does not fit the rhyming scheme as translated) means something like "dark horse" or "black horse". The proper name "Black" is unknown in the histories of the ancient world. But there are oblique references to "shadows" that are not the common undead shadows, and one or two references to a "shadow of a black horse", or possibly a "black dog" that seems to have had prodigious power, though what that power was is also unknown. It is possible that Kulakoonstru's human companion Mahatmas had somehow made the acquaintance of a being such as this and was thus able to call upon it during his time of great need. No other reference to this creature exists in any known scientific or historical literature.

Hoping for his friend to arrive.
Though at risk of great mortal harms,
The Awesome One Kulakoonstru,
With all four of his mighty arms,
Dueled to come back safely through.
He struggled to break from shadow,
With the prize of the precious throne,
And so with his great might unbowed,
Kulakoonstru battles alone
'Gainst the evil, vile, putrid king.
He fights and drags the prize back home,
Fulfilling now the quest to bring
The chair to the Arkoth dungeon.
The man declares when they arrive:
"I gave you near one chance in three
"To complete this task and survive
"And return this relic to me!"
All Kulakoonstru's eyes widened,
Mahatmas' mouth dropped open.
The two then heavily sighed and
Left their own mind's thoughts unspoken.
The smiling man was very pleased,
He was well and truly amazed,
That the companions had achieved
Such a difficult task, unfazed.
But the brave duo are granted
Only few adequate rewards,
For the massive risks demanded
And the grave dangers untowards.
No vexation their faces showed,
They accepted with solemn grace
The meager bounty then bestowed,
Never to return to that place.

Kulakoonstru! Kulakoonstru!
Diamond Wielder! Tech Wielder!
Ability Wielder! Lithon Wielder!
Supplier of Clarth's Petroni!
Close, Personal Friend of the Death God!
The Unseen! Time Traveler!
Shadow Walker! The Good!
Lord of Yaninas! LORD OF YANINAS!

XVII

This is another canto that is almost completely missing. There are very limited fragments of verse intact. Barely enough to make out a general outline of what happens. Kulakoonstru and Mahatmas go to the Elven dungeon again, but this time they go to the much more mysterious second level. This level appears to be on a different plane than the other two known levels, this knowledge is new to scholars of our time.

Several adventures ensue, with battles and treasure acquisition. One thing that stands out is a battle with one of the Trinali[45], Kulakoonstru was apparently able to defeat this creature with his technology based weapons.

There is not even enough verse to publish from this canto. The ending is, however, delineated by the refrain of titles (omitted in this case as redundant), and there are the above references to the Elven dungeon and Trinali, but nothing that can be presented.

---

[45] Trinali are viscous and evil undead sorcerers, that are generally immune to most magic. See: Undeads of This Plane and Others, vol. 5, 2nd Ed. By Shurmurolon, University of Arqnasquirg Press, p291 - 328.

XVIII

There are only a few fragments from Canto XVIII. But it seems like quite a bit happened during this adventure. Kulakoonstru and Mahatmas (and apparently some others) went back to the Demon Dungeon, where some very unfortunate things befell Kulakoonstru.

...{missing}
Statue of The Asshole being
Tormented, grimacing in pain.
Everyone there began laughing,
Mirth rolled out, again and again!
They chuckled as they left the room,
Coming to a small, pitch dark space.
Kulakoonstru entered the gloom,
Returned full of evil menace!
And an even worse change happened:
He was worshipping The Asshole!
Frantic, Mahatmas called Clarth in,
Who knocked Kulakoonstru out cold.
His True Flame was strangely remade,
To fix it required great skill.
Clarth knew just who to call for aid.
He drew a card[46] and bent his will,
A huge glowing red orb appeared!
It was the King of Rakshasa.
Clarth bowed and Mahatmas then cheered,
The King could fix this hateful flaw!
In their minds did they hear him speak,
"O! Great Clarth, what is now your need?"

---

[46] cf. The summary for Canto IX for a description of what this card Clarth used may have been.

"My friend has been cursed, things are bleak,
"Can you help? I'd be glad indeed!"
"I can change his True Flame today.
"But alignment must be reversed,
"To keep Asshole Demon away.
"So he will be no longer be cursed".
And to his word the King was true,
He restored him to how he should.
So he is back! Kulakoonstru
Is now and e'er known as: The Good!

Kulakoonstru! Kulakoonstru!
Diamond Wielder! Tech Wielder!
Ability Wielder! Lithon Wielder!
Supplier of Clarth's Petroni!
Close, Personal Friend of the Death God!
The Unseen! Time Traveler!
Shadow Walker! The Good!
Lord of Yaninas! LORD OF YANINAS!

XIX

For Canto XIX, which is the last canto, there are only a very few fragments that can be deciphered or reconstructed. It is clear that Kulakoonstru had some stupendous adventures throughout the planes of existence during this period, and seemed to have gained at least two new titles during this time.

Based on external evidence, it would appear he was gone from our plane for nearly 80 years. But, as I understand it, time moves differently on the different planes, so the elapsed time for Kulakoonstru was likely much less.

He also seems to have had a rather special item created for himself, an item which would permanently supply him (and others) with Yanina beer. While that is not unusual (this is a fairly common item for Yaninas, even in our time - I have one myself) what seems to be special about it is that it was crafted using power from one of the highest known planes of existence and consequently would likely work anywhere, possibly even in today's time with chi based magic, though that hypothesis has not been tested.

...{missing}
He bravely endured many trials,
From plane to plane he went and more!
Now has added to his titles:
For he is now Plane Traveler!
He reached the goal of his journey,
Reaching the mystic Elven plane,
"Here I have now arrived," said he
"At the wondrous Elven domain!"
A special favor he did ask:
Would the Elves use magic to make,
A wondrous Yanina beer flask?
They did, now his thirst he could slake!

...{missing}...
His plane traveling came to an end,
There was exciting news, because,
There's a new Close, Personal Friend:
The great King of The Rakshasas!

Kulakoonstru! Kulakoonstru!
Diamond Wielder! Tech Wielder!
Ability Wielder! Lithon Wielder!
Supplier of Clarth's Petroni!

Close, Personal Friend of the Death God!
The Unseen! Time Traveler!
Shadow Walker! The Good!
Lord of Yaninas! LORD OF YANINAS!

This is the end of the scrolls that I discovered in the chest in Arqnasquirg those many years ago. I have endeavored to present them as they were originally intended, although through the translations, much nuance regarding Kulakoonstru's remarkable life has probably been lost.

The original scrolls are now housed in a magically sustained stasis in the archives at the University of Airë Silanarfarnë. They are available for limited study and examination by serious Kulakoonstru scholars, upon successful application to the curator.

Appendix

The Titles of Kulakoonstru

For the titles listed in the canto refrain, the acquisition of all of them are in the text of the ballad. The astute reader will discern these titles as they are explained. But for reference, I include the text locations here, in the order given in the refrain:

- Diamond Wielder - Canto III - line 240
- Tech Wielder - Canto VI - line 651
- Ability Wielder - Canto III - line 222
- Lithon Wielder - Canto IV - line 330
- Supplier Of Clarth's Petroni - Canto VII - line 818
- Close, Personal Friend of the Death God - Canto IV - line 404
- The Unseen - Canto XIV - line 1194
- Time Traveler - Canto XV - line 1234
- Shadow Walker - Canto XVI - line 1314
- The Good - Canto XVIII - line 1474

As mentioned in the preface, not all of Kulakoonstru's titles are part of the refrain. There are several more that are known from the existence of the cylinder seal that was discovered in situ with the scrolls. I present them all here for reference, as they would have been displayed by applying the seal:

- Ability Wielder
- Diamond Wielder
- Lithon Wielder
- Close, Personal Friend of the Death God
- Tech Wielder
- The Unseen
- Time Traveler
- The Good

- Shadow Walker
- Plane Walker
- Close, Personal Friend of the King of The Rakshasas
- Necromancer[47]
- Supplier Of Clarth's Petroni
- Pattern Walker
- Plane Traveler
- Lord Of Yaninas[48]

---

[47] This title is totally mysterious. No reference to Kulakoonstru being a necromancer or controlling undead is extant in the scrolls. It only appears on the cylinder seal. It is possible that this occurred after the composition of the scroll, but prior to Kulakoonstru departing these planes, leaving his cylinder seal behind.

[48] Regarding the title: "Lord of Yaninas", this title is supported by independent sources in various private and scholarly libraries in Arqnasquirg and elsewhere. While there is no indication that Kulakoonstru was a member of the Royal Family, it does appear that he was, in fact, of somewhat noble birth and it is entirely possible that he would have been referred to as a "Lord of Yaninas". Certainly his exploits as an adventurer would entitle him to this honor.

Afterword and Acknowledgements (2nd Ed.)

The study of Kulakoonstru is a very rewarding field of research, and this group of scrolls has been one of the most important documents regarding this famous Yanina. The research is ongoing, but I believe that what I have presented here is essentially the most complete version of the Ballad of Kulakoonstru, and as such, is the most definitive history of his remarkable life.

I would like to acknowledge the invaluable assistance from the following distinguished scholars and priests.

At the main temple of Silanarë in Arqnasquirg, the High Priest, Olorshinikulu, offered their unreserved support for my research in to the life of the remarkable Kulakoonstru. Without this support, this work would not have been possible.

Also, assisting with translating the ancient Yanina language were the following acolytes: Avuinkurana, Hiliserkutun, Uakulakur, Estonomotolopuru and Thrankurorp. These Yaninas were invaluable in the early translation work, tracking down reference volumes and other ancient scrolls with example texts in them as well. My undying gratitude to them.

As the work progressed, research was conducted at the University of Airë Silanarfarnë, where both the university president, Wurlurntrikolu, and my immediate predecessor as the Chair of the Department of Kulakoonstru Studies, Querinstrunun, provided their support and research assistance during the long period of research into the scrolls.

I would also like to mention several of the very helpful human scholars and priests, especially Werin Stirn, lead scholar of ancient studies at the temple of Silanarë in Old Arbeneth, who was instrumental in tracking down several important scrolls from the ancient temple of the Death God, which were used to fill in some of the gaps in Canto IV. And Hulas Therims, High Priest at the temple of Silanarë in Old Arbeneth. Without their assistance, we would know less about how Kulakoonstru became the Close, Personal Friend of the Death God.

Most of all, I would like to thank our great Silanarë, who is the shining light in the darkness of this world. Thank you! I would like to offer up this prayer to him:

"O Great and Holy Silanarë, we beseech you to shine Your Ginormous Light upon our unworthy heads, so that we may lift up our countenances and be blessed!"

Selected Bibliography

There are a wide variety of sources used in the preparation of this work. Following is a selected list of important sources.

Aklorhuru. *Four Thousand Yanina Beers To Try Before You Die.* Sinfilu Bros. Publishing.

_____. *Regional Yanina Breweries.* Beer Books Of Arqnasquirg.

_____. *The Best Local Craft Yanina Beers.* Sinfilu Bros. Publishing.

_____. *Where Is The Best Yanina Beer Brewed?*. Arqnasquirg Biblio.

Ashurordos. Maclenuru Tasting Notes (Sample #20310). *Squirg Yesterday And Today*, vol. I, issue 8, pp. 17-20. Institute For Squirg Studies

Bilistra, Codi. *Important Artifacts of the Pre-Splinter Epoch.* University of Arberneth Publishing.

Dositrokulik. *The Fulirdrage Range.* Institute For Squirg Studies.

Faln, Orif. *What Was "Mana"?* Arberneth College Of Magic.

Fealirumkin. Heresy Exposed: Mixing Squirg With Common Beverages. *Squirg Yesterday And Today,* vol. II, issue 25, pp. 8-19. Institute For Squirg Studies

Feilsuroro, Bruniurru & Glorgino. Kulakoonstru's Human Companions. *Journal Of Kulakoonstru*

Studies, vol. 104, issue 9, pp. 1-44. University of Arqnasquirg Press

Fikurnoalin. *Maclenuru: Myth or Real?* Institute For Squirg Studies.

_____. *Modern vs. Ancient Squirg.* Institute For Squirg Studies.

Filstonookin. *Brew Pubs of Arqnasquirg.* Arqnasquirg Biblio.

Foaleskola. *Seeking Maclenuru: A Guide.* Holy Silanarë Press, Ltd. (Arqnasquirg).

Garshar, Ocen (Ed.). *The Quasi-Planes.* Arberneth College Of Magic.

Goristruluru. *Hops! They Matter To Yanina Beer.* Sinfilu Bros. Publishing.

Halugaru (Ed.). *Ancient Yanina Language Glossary (6th ed.).* University of Arqnasquirg Press.

Harnes, Yorics. Ancient Yanina. Is it a Real Language? *Journal Of Precursor Languages*, vol. 58, issue 7, pp. 6-12. University of Arberneth Publishing

Horishutoul. *How Much Yanina Beer Can You Drink?* Beer Books Of Arqnasquirg.

Hosee, Lirin. *Lithon: The Elven Metal.* University of Arberneth Publishing.

Husuvros. *Yanina Beer Making Handbook.* Holy Silanarë Press, Ltd. (Arqnasquirg).

Husuvros. *Make Mine Yanina Beer!* Beer Books Of Arqnasquirg.

Ikulirbunus. *The Five Regions of Squirg.* Holy Silanarë Press, Ltd. (Arqnasquirg).

Imisururoi. What Is A "True-Titan"? *Journal Of Kulakoonstru Studies,* vol. 78, issue 12, pp. 4-13. University of Arqnasquirg Press

Inunurru et. al.. A Survey Of Kulakoonstru's Known Diamonds. *Journal Of Kulakoonstru Studies,* vol. 44, issue 8, pp. 3-29. University of Arqnasquirg Press

Jirakusturu. *Yeasts And Their Impact On Yanina Beer.* The Yanina Beer Academy.

Jusinrequu. *An Archeological History Of Arqnasquirg.* University of Arqnasquirg Press.

Karnif, Gorisar. *Gods of Ancient Times.* College Of Religious Studies.

Koarfirtudu. *Squirg Tasting Notes.* Holy Silanarë Press, Ltd. (Arqnasquirg).

Korisandouli et. al.. Is Stasis Storage of Maclenuru Acceptable? *Squirg Yesterday And Today,* vol. I, issue 7, pp. 12-141. Institute For Squirg Studies

Kurlarnunu. *Pour Another (Sampling Yanina Beers).* Beer Books Of Arqnasquirg.

Lorusunnur. *Yanina Beer And The Influence On World History.* The Yanina Beer Academy.

Lurerflidoo & Rurinbro. *Heirloom Yanina Beers.* The Yanina Beer Academy.

_____. *Legendary Yanina Brews.* The Yanina Beer Academy.

_____. *Recreating Ancient Yanina Beers.* The Yanina Beer Academy.

Marustrufoko. *Using Science and Magic To Make Better Yanina Beer.* The Yanina Beer Academy.

none. *Yanina Squirg: How To Safely Imbibe.* Old Aberneth Government Publication.

Noribordulu. Maclenuru Tasting Notes (Sample #80754). *Squirg Yesterday And Today,* vol. IV, issue 14, pp. 102-103. Institute For Squirg Studies

Nosathironu & Horkoruluu. *Yaninas In The Pre-Silanarë Universe.* University of Arqnasquirg Press.

Nosathironu et. al.. Ancient Yanina Populations Throughout Human Lands. *Annals Of Yanina History,* vol. 8, issue 2, pp. 34-80. University of Arqnasquirg Press

Okolrku. Sharalaca and Kulakoonstru, Not Close, Personal Friends. *Journal Of Kulakoonstru Studies,* vol. 33, issue 3, pp. 11-25. University of Arqnasquirg Press

Oruduinst (Ed.). *The Squirg Masters Of Yaninaland.* Institute For Squirg Studies.

Piruskuwilor. *Famous Closed Squirg Distilleries.* Holy Silanarë Press, Ltd. (Arqnasquirg).

Querinstrunun. Was Kulakoonstru A "Lord Of Yaninas"? *Journal Of Kulakoonstru Studies,* vol. 18, issue 8, pp. 10-18. University of Arqnasquirg Press

Querinstrunun & Ukunhururarklo. Kulakoonstru's Impact On Yaninaland. *Annals Of Yanina History,* vol. 21, issue 3, pp. 1-132. University of Arqnasquirg Press

Rodularkosuu. *The Non-Yanina Races (4th ed.).* University of Arqnasquirg Press.

Sarunu & Teilina. Kulakoonstru's Ever Changing Alignment. *Journal Of Kulakoonstru Studies,* vol. 80, issue 7, pp. 91-104. University of Arqnasquirg Press

Scrimoruluk. Historical Availability of Maclenuru. *Squirg Yesterday And Today,* vol. I, issue 17, pp. 70-91. Institute For Squirg Studies

Shurmurolon. *Undeads of This Plane and Others (2nd ed.).* University of Arqnasquirg Press.

Simirlon, Orofust & Glasonur. *The Complete Yanina Beer Course.* The Yanina Beer Academy.

Sirturdinu. *Sirturdinu's Squirg Hunter's Guide.* Sinfilu Bros. Publishing.

_____. *The Beginners Guide To Squirg.* Sinfilu Bros. Publishing.

Sokomroaru (Ed.). *Encyclopedia of Yanina Beer.* The Yanina Beer Academy.

Stirn, Werin. Demon Languages of Hell. *Journal Of Precursor Languages,* vol. 34, issue 1, pp. 81-224. University of Arberneth Publishing

_____. *Translating Ancient Languages (2nd ed.).* University of Arberneth Publishing.

_____ (Ed.). *Friends Of The Death God (Reprinted).* Holy Silanarë Press, Ltd. (Arberneth).

Supahorturn & Fikurnoalin. *The History of Squirg.* Institute For Squirg Studies.

Ukunhururarklo. *Kulakoonstru: A Brief History (2nd ed.).* Holy Silanarë Press, Ltd. (Arqnasquirg).

_____. Speculation on Kulakoonstru's Ultimate Fate. *Journal Of Kulakoonstru Studies,* vol. 125, issue 1, pp. 1-24. University of Arqnasquirg Press

_____. The Legend Of Clarth's Companions. *Journal Of Kulakoonstru Studies,* vol. 27, issue 9, pp. 1-18. University of Arqnasquirg Press

_____. What Happened To Kulakoonstru's Dragon? *Journal Of Kulakoonstru Studies,* vol. 60, issue 4, pp. 31-49. University of Arqnasquirg Press

Ukunhururarklo & Hosee L. Petroni: A Study. *Journal Of Kulakoonstru Studies,* vol. 91, issue 6, pp. 82-143. University of Arqnasquirg Press

Visinorde, Farrin (Ed.). *Known Dungeons in Ancient Ages.* Arberneth College Of Magic.

Wrorlunofo. *Aging Squirg: A Handbook.* The Squirg Producers Guild.

Index

www.ingramcontent.com/pod-product-compliance
Lightning Source LLC
Chambersburg PA
CBHW010758310726
48980CB00008B/816/J
9781614690696